The Rector by Margaret Oliphant

Margaret Oliphant Wilson was born on April 4th, 1828 to Francis W. Wilson, a clerk, and Margaret Oliphant, at Wallyford, near Musselburgh, East Lothian.

Her youth was spent in establishing a writing style and by 1849 she had her first novel published: Passages in the Life of Mrs. Margaret Maitland.

Two years later, in 1851 Caleb Field was published and also an invitation to contribute to Blackwood's Magazine; the beginning of a life time business relationship.

In May 1852, Margaret married her cousin, Frank Wilson Oliphant. Their marriage produced six children but, tragically, three died in infancy. When her husband developed signs of the dreaded consumption (tuberculosis) they moved to Florence, and then to Rome where, sadly, he died.

Margaret was naturally devastated but was also now left without support and only her income from writing to support the family. She returned to England and took up the burden of supporting her three remaining children by her literary activity.

Her incredible and prolific work rate increased both her commercial reputation and the size of her reading audience. Tragedy struck again in January 1864 when her only remaining daughter Maggie died.

In 1866 she settled at Windsor to be closer to her sons, who were being educated at near-by Eton School.

For more than thirty years she pursued a varied literary career but family life continued to bring problems. Cyril Francis, her eldest son, died in 1890. The younger son, Francis, who she nicknamed 'Cecco', died in 1894.

With the last of her children now lost to her, she had little further interest in life. Her health steadily and inexorably declined.

Margaret Oliphant Wilson Oliphant died at the age of 69 in Wimbledon on 20th June 1897. She is buried in Eton beside her sons.

Index of Contents

CHAPTER I

It is natural to suppose that the arrival of the new Rector was a rather exciting event for Carlingford. It is a considerable town, it is true, nowadays, but then there are no alien activities to disturb the place—no manufactures, and not much trade. And there is a very respectable amount of very good society at Carlingford. To begin with, it is a pretty place—mild, sheltered, not far from town; and naturally its very reputation for good society increases the amount of that much-prized article. The advantages of the town in this respect have already put five per cent upon the house-rents; but this, of course, only refers to the real town, where you can go through an entire street of high garden-walls, with houses inside full of the retired exclusive comforts, the dainty economical refinement peculiar to such places; and where the good people consider their own society as a warrant of gentility less splendid, but not less assured, than the favour of Majesty itself. Naturally there are no Dissenters in Carlingford—that is to say, none above the rank of a greengrocer or milkman; and in bosoms devoted to the Church it may be well imagined that the advent of the new Rector was an event full of importance, and even of excitement.

He was highly spoken of, everybody knew; but nobody knew who had spoken highly of him, nor had been able to find out, even by inference, what were his views. The Church had been Low during the last Rector's reign—profoundly Low—lost in the deepest abysses of Evangelicalism. A determined inclination to preach to everybody had seized upon that good man's brain; he had half emptied Salem Chapel, there could be no doubt; but, on the other hand, he had more than half filled the Chapel of St Roque, half a mile out of Carlingford, where the perpetual curate, young, handsome, and fervid, was on the very topmost pinnacle of Anglicanism. St Roque's was not more than a pleasant walk from the best quarter of Carlingford, on the north side of the town, thank heaven! which one could get at without the dread passage of that new horrid suburb, to which young Mr Rider, the young doctor, was devoting himself. But the Evangelical rector was dead, and his reign was over, and nobody could predict what the character of the new administration was to be. The obscurity in which the new Rector had buried his views was the most extraordinary thing about him. He had taken high honours at college, and was "highly spoken of;" but whether he was High, or Low, or Broad, muscular or sentimental, sermonising or decorative, nobody in the world seemed able to tell.

"Fancy if he were just to be a Mr Bury over again! Fancy him going to the canal, and having sermons to the bargemen, and attending to all sorts of people except to us, whom it is his duty to attend to!" cried one of this much-canvassed clergyman's curious parishioners. "Indeed I do believe he must be one of these people. If he were in society at all, somebody would be sure to know."

"Lucy dear, Mr Bury christened you," said another not less curious but more tolerant inquirer.

"Then he did you the greatest of all services," cried the third member of the little group which discussed the new Rector under Mr Wodehouse's blossomed apple-trees. "He conferred such a benefit upon you that he deserves all reverence at your hand. Wonderful idea! a man confers this greatest of Christian blessings on multitudes, and does not himself appreciate the boon he conveys!"

"Well, for that matter, Mr Wentworth, you know—" said the elder lady; but she got no farther. Though she was verging upon forty, leisurely, pious, and unmarried, that good Miss Wodehouse was not polemical. She had "her own opinions," but few people knew much about them. She was seated on a green garden-bench which surrounded the great May-tree in that large, warm, well-furnished garden. The high brick walls, all clothed with fruit-trees, shut in an enclosure of which not a morsel except this velvet grass, with its nests of daisies, was not under the highest and most careful cultivation. It was such a scene as is only to be found in an old country town; the walls jealous of intrusion, yet thrusting tall plumes of lilac and stray branches of apple-blossom, like friendly salutations to the world without; within, the blossoms drooping over the light bright head of Lucy Wodehouse underneath the apple-trees, and impertinently flecking the Rev. Frank Wentworth's Anglican coat. These two last were young people, with that indefinable harmony in their looks which prompts the suggestion of "a handsome couple" to the bystander. It had not even occurred to them to be in love with each other, so far as anybody knew, yet few were the undiscerning persons who saw them together without instinctively placing the young curate of St Roque's in permanence by Lucy's side. She was twenty, pretty, blue-eyed, and full of dimples, with a broad Leghorn hat thrown carelessly on her head, untied, with broad strings of blue ribbon falling among her fair curls—a blue which was "repeated," according to painter jargon, in ribbons at her throat and waist. She had great gardening gloves on, and a basket and huge pair of scissors on the grass at her feet, which grass, besides, was strewed with a profusion of all the sweetest spring blossoms—the sweet narcissus, most exquisite of flowers, lilies of the valley, white and blue hyacinths, golden ranunculus globes—worlds of sober, deep-breathing wallflower. If Lucy had been doing what her kind elder sister called her "duty," she would have been at this moment arranging her flowers in the drawing-room; but the times were rare when Lucy did her duty according to Miss Wodehouse's estimate; so instead of arranging those clusters of narcissus, she clubbed them together in her hands into a fragrant dazzling sheaf, and discussed the new Rector—not unaware, perhaps, in her secret heart, that the sweet morning, the sunshine and flowers, and exhilarating air, were somehow secretly enhanced by the presence of that black Anglican figure under the apple-trees.

"But I suppose," said Lucy, with a sigh, "we must wait till we see him; and if I must be very respectful of Mr Bury because he christened me, I am heartily glad the new Rector has no claim upon my reverence. I have been christened, I have been confirmed—"

"But, Lucy, my dear, the chances are he will marry you," said Miss Wodehouse, calmly; "indeed, there can be no doubt that it is only natural he should, for he is the Rector, you know; and though we go so often to St Roque's, Mr Wentworth will excuse me saying that he is a very young man."

Miss Wodehouse was knitting; she did not see the sudden look of dismay and amazement which the curate of St Roque's darted down upon her, nor the violent sympathetic blush which blazed over both the young faces. How shocking that elderly quiet people should have such a faculty for suggestions! You may be sure Lucy Wodehouse and young Wentworth, had it not been "put into their heads" in such an absurd fashion, would never, all their virtuous lives, have dreamt of anything but friendship. Deep silence ensued after this simple but startling speech. Miss Wodehouse knitted on, and took no notice; Lucy began to gather up the flowers into the basket, unable for her life to think of anything to say. For his part, Mr Wentworth gravely picked the apple-blossoms off his coat, and counted them in his hand. That sweet summer snow kept dropping, dropping, falling here and there as the wind carried it, and with a special attraction to Lucy and her blue ribbons; while behind, Miss Wodehouse sat calmly on the green bench, under the May-tree just beginning to bloom, without lifting her eyes from her knitting. Not far off, the bright English house, all beaming with open doors and windows, shone in the sunshine. With the white May peeping out among the green overhead, and the sweet narcissus in a great dazzling sheaf upon the grass, making all the air fragrant around them, can anybody fancy a sweeter domestic out-of-door scene? or else it seemed so to the perpetual curate of St Roque's.

Ah me! and if he was to be perpetual curate, and none of his great friends thought upon him, or had preferment to bestow, how do you suppose he could ever, ever marry Lucy Wodehouse, if they were to wait a hundred years?

Just then the garden-gate—the green gate in the wall—opened to the creaking murmur of Mr Wodehouse's own key. Mr Wodehouse was a man who creaked universally. His boots were a heavy infliction upon the good-humour of his household; and like every other invariable quality of dress, the peculiarity became identified with him in every particular of his life. Everything belonging to him moved with a certain jar, except, indeed, his household, which went on noiseless wheels, thanks to Lucy and love. As he came along the garden path, the gravel started all round his unmusical foot. Miss Wodehouse alone turned round to hail her father's approach, but both the young people looked up at her instinctively, and saw her little start, the falling of her knitting-needles, the little flutter of colour which surprise brought to her maidenly, middle-aged cheek. How they both divined it I cannot tell, but it certainly was no surprise to either of them when a tall embarrassed figure, following the portly one of Mr Wodehouse, stepped suddenly from the noisy gravel to the quiet grass, and stood gravely awkward behind the father of the house.

"My dear children, here's the Rector—delighted to see him! we're all delighted to see him!" cried Mr Wodehouse. "This is my little girl Lucy, and this is my eldest daughter. They're both as good as curates, though I say it, you know, as shouldn't. I suppose you've got something tidy for lunch, Lucy, eh? To be sure you ought to know—how can I tell? She might have had only cold mutton, for anything I knew—and that won't do, you know, after college fare. Hollo, Wentworth! I beg your pardon—who thought of seeing you here? I thought you had morning service, and all that sort of thing. Delighted to make you known to the Rector so soon. Mr Proctor—Mr Wentworth of St Roque's."

The Rector bowed. He had no time to say anything, fortunately for him; but a vague sort of colour fluttered over his face. It was his first living; and cloistered in All-Souls for fifteen years of his life, how is a man to know all at once how to accost his parishioners? especially when these curious unknown specimens of natural life happen to be female creatures, doubtless accustomed to compliment and civility. If ever any one was thankful to hear the sound of another man's voice, that person was the new Rector of Carlingford, standing in the bewildering garden-scene into which the green door had so suddenly admitted him, all but treading on the dazzling bundle of narcissus, and turning with embarrassed politeness from the perpetual curate, whose salutation was less cordial than it might have been, to those indefinite flutters of blue ribbon from which Mr Proctor's tall figure divided the ungracious young man.

"But come along to lunch. Bless me! don't let us be too ceremonious," cried Mr Wodehouse. "Take Lucy, my dear sir—take Lucy. Though she has her garden-gloves on, she's manager indoors for all that. Molly here is the one we coddle up and take care of. Put down your knitting, child, and don't make an old woman of yourself. To be sure, it's your own concern—you should know best; but that's my opinion. Why, Wentworth, where are you off to? 'Tisn't a fast, surely—is it, Mary?—nothing of the sort; it's Thursday—Thursday, do you hear? and the Rector newly arrived. Come along."

"I am much obliged, but I have an appointment," began the curate, with restraint.

"Why didn't you keep it, then, before we came in," cried Mr Wodehouse, "chatting with a couple of girls like Lucy and Mary? Come along, come along—an appointment with some old woman or other, who wants to screw flannels and things out of you—well, I suppose so! I don't know anything else you could have to say to them. Come along."

"Thank you. I shall hope to wait on the Rector shortly," said young Wentworth, more and more stiffly; "but at present I am sorry it is not in my power. Good morning, Miss Wodehouse—good morning; I am happy to have had the opportunity—" and the voice of the perpetual curate died off into vague murmurs of politeness as he made his way towards the green door.

That green door! what a slight, paltry barrier—one plank and no more; but outside a dusty dry road, nothing to be seen but other high brick walls, with here and there an apple-tree or a lilac, or the half-developed flower-turrets of a chestnut looking over—nothing to be seen but a mean little costermonger's cart, with a hapless donkey, and, down in the direction of St Roque's, the long road winding, still drier and dustier. Ah me! was it paradise inside? or was it only a merely mortal lawn dropped over with apple-blossoms, blue ribbons, and other vanities? Who could tell? The perpetual curate wended sulky on his way. I fear the old woman would have made neither flannel nor tea and sugar out of him in that inhuman frame of mind.

"Dreadful young prig that young Wentworth," said Mr Wodehouse, "but comes of a great family, you know, and gets greatly taken notice of—to be sure he does, child. I suppose it's for his family's sake: I can't see into people's hearts. It may be higher motives, to be sure, and all that. He's gone off in a huff about something; never mind, luncheon comes up all the same. Now, let's address ourselves to the business of life."

For when Mr Wodehouse took knife and fork in hand a singular result followed. He was silent—at least he talked no longer: the mystery of carving, of eating, of drinking—all the serious business of the table—engrossed the good man. He had nothing more to say for the moment; and then a dread unbroken silence fell upon the little company. The Rector coloured, faltered, cleared his throat—he had not an idea how to get into conversation with such unknown entities. He looked hard at Lucy, with a bold intention of addressing her; but, having the bad fortune to meet her eye, shrank back, and withdrew the venture. Then the good man inclined his profile towards Miss Wentworth. His eyes wandered wildly round the room in search of a suggestion; but, alas! it was a mere dining-room, very comfortable, but not imaginative. In his dreadful dilemma he was infinitely relieved by the sound of somebody's voice.

"I trust you will like Carlingford, Mr Proctor," said Miss Wodehouse, mildly.

"Yes—oh yes; I trust so," answered the confused but grateful man; "that is, it will depend very much, of course, on the kind of people I find here."

"Well, we are a little vain. To tell the truth, indeed, we rather pride ourselves a little on the good society in Carlingford," said his gentle and charitable interlocutor.

"Ah, yes—ladies?" said the Rector: "hum—that was not what I was thinking of."

"But, oh, Mr Proctor," cried Lucy, with a sudden access of fun, "you don't mean to say that you dislike ladies' society, I hope?"

The Rector gave an uneasy half-frightened glance at her. The creature was dangerous even to a Fellow of All-Souls.

"I may say I know very little about them," said the bewildered clergyman. As soon as he had said the words he thought they sounded rude; but how could he help it?—the truth of his speech was indisputable.

"Come here, and we'll initiate you—come here as often as you can spare us a little of your time," cried Mr Wodehouse, who had come to a pause in his operations. "You couldn't have a better chance. They're head people in Carlingford, though I say it. There's Mary, she's a learned woman; take you up in a false quantity, sir, a deal sooner than I should. And Lucy, she's in another line altogether; but there's quantities of people swear by her. What's the matter, children, eh? I suppose so—people tell me so. If people tell me so all day long, I'm entitled to believe it, I presume?"

Lucy answered this by a burst of laughter, not loud but cordial, which rang sweet and strange upon the Rector's ears. Miss Wodehouse, on the contrary, looked a little ashamed, blushed a pretty pink old-maidenly blush, and mildly remonstrated with papa. The whole scene was astonishing to the stranger. He had been living out of nature so long that he wondered within himself whether it was common to retain the habits and words of childhood to such an age as that which good Miss Wodehouse put no disguise upon, or if sisters with twenty years of difference between them were usual in ordinary households. He looked at them with looks which to Miss Wodehouse appeared disapproving, but which in reality meant only surprise and discomfort. He was exceedingly glad when lunch was over, and he was at liberty to take his leave. With very different feelings from those of young Wentworth the Rector crossed the boundary of that green door. When he saw it closed behind him he drew a long breath of relief, and looked up and down the dusty road, and through those lines of garden walls, where the loads of blossom burst over everywhere, with a sensation of having escaped and got at liberty. After a momentary pause and gaze round him in enjoyment of that liberty, the Rector gave a start and went on again rapidly. A dismayed, discomfited, helpless sensation came over him. These parishioners!—these female parishioners! From out of another of those green doors had just emerged a brilliant group of ladies, the rustle of whose dress and murmur of whose voices he could hear in the genteel half-rural silence. The Rector bolted: he never slackened pace nor drew breath till he was safe in the vacant library of the Rectory, among old Mr Bury's book-shelves. It seemed the only safe place in Carlingford to the languishing transplanted Fellow of All-Souls.

CHAPTER II

A month later, Mr Proctor had got fairly settled in his new rectory, with a complete modest establishment becoming his means—for Carlingford was a tolerable living. And in the newly-furnished sober drawing-room sat a very old lady, lively but infirm, who was the Rector's mother. Nobody knew that this old woman kept the Fellow of All-Souls still a boy at heart, nor that the reserved and inappropriate man forgot his awkwardness in his mother's presence. He was not only a very affectionate son, but a dutiful good child to her. It had been his pet scheme for years to bring her from her Devonshire cottage, and make her mistress of his house. That had been the chief attraction, indeed, which drew him to Carlingford; for had he consulted his own tastes, and kept to his college, who would insure him that at seventy-five his old mother might not glide away out of life without that last gleam of sunshine long intended for her by her grateful son?

This scene, accordingly, was almost the only one which reconciled him to the extraordinary change in his life. There she sat, the lively old lady; very deaf, as you could almost divine by that vivid inquiring twinkle in her eyes; feeble too, for she had a silver-headed cane beside her chair, and even with that assistance seldom moved across the room when she could help it. Feeble in body, but alert in mind, ready to read anything, to hear anything, to deliver her opinions freely; resting in her big chair in the complete repose of age, gratified with her son's attentions, and over-joyed in his company; interested about everything, and as ready to enter into all the domestic concerns of the new people as if she had lived all her life among them. The Rector sighed and smiled as he listened to his mother's questions, and did his best, at the top of his voice, to enlighten her. His mother was, let us say, a hundred years or so younger than the Rector. If she had been his bride, and at the blithe commencement of life, she could not have shown more inclination to know all about Carlingford. Mr Proctor was middle-aged, and preoccupied by right of his years; but his mother had long ago got over that stage of life. She was at that point when some energetic natures, having got to the bottom of the hill, seem to make a fresh start and re-ascend. Five years ago, old Mrs Proctor had completed the human term; now she had recommenced her life.

But, to tell the very truth, the Rector would very fain, had that been possible, have confined her inquiries to books and public affairs. For to make confidential disclosures, either concerning one's self or other people, in a tone of voice perfectly audible in the kitchen, is somewhat trying. He had become acquainted with those dread parishioners of his during this interval. Already they had worn him to death with dinner-parties—dinner-parties very pleasant and friendly, when one got used to them; but to a stranger frightful reproductions of each other, with the same dishes, the same dresses, the same stories, in which the Rector communicated gravely with his next neighbour, and eluded as long as he could those concluding moments in the drawing-room which were worst of all. It cannot be said that his parishioners made much progress in their knowledge of the Rector. What his "views" were, nobody could divine any more than they could before his arrival. He made no innovations whatever; but he did not pursue Mr Bury's Evangelical ways, and never preached a sermon or a word more than was absolutely necessary. When zealous Churchmen discussed the progress of Dissent, the Rector scarcely looked interested; and nobody could move him to express an opinion concerning all that lovely upholstery with which Mr Wentworth had decorated St Roque's. People asked in vain, what was he? He was neither High nor Low, enlightened nor narrow-minded; he was a Fellow of All-Souls.

"But now tell me, my dear," said old Mrs Proctor, "who's Mr Wodehouse?"

With despairing calmness, the Rector approached his voice to her ear. "He's a churchwarden!" cried the unfortunate man, in a shrill whisper.

"He's what?—you forget I don't hear very well. I'm a great deal deafer, Morley, my dear, than I was the last time you were in Devonshire. What did you say Mr Wodehouse was?"

"He's an ass!" exclaimed the baited Rector.

Mrs Proctor nodded her head with a great many little satisfied assenting nods.

"Exactly my own opinion, my dear. What I like in your manner of expressing yourself, Morley, is its conciseness," said the laughing old lady. "Just so—exactly what I imagined; but being an ass, you know, doesn't account for him coming here so often. What is he besides, my dear?"

The Rector made spasmodic gestures towards the door, to the great amusement of his lively mother; and then produced, with much confusion and after a long search, his pocketbook, on a leaf of paper in which he wrote—loudly, in big characters—"He's a churchwarden—they'll hear in the kitchen."

"He's a churchwarden! And what if they do hear in the kitchen?" cried the old lady, greatly amused; "it isn't a sin. Well, now, let me hear: has he a family, Morley?"

Again Mr Proctor showed a little discomposure. After a troubled look at the door, and pause, as if he meditated a remonstrance, he changed his mind, and answered, "Two daughters!" shouting sepulchrally into his mother's ear.

"Oh so!" cried the old lady—"two daughters—so, so—that explains it all at once. I know now why he comes to the Rectory so often. And, I declare, I never thought of it before. Why, you're always there!—so, so—and he's got two daughters, has he? To be sure; now I understand it all."

The Rector looked helpless and puzzled. It was difficult to take the initiative and ask why—but the poor man looked so perplexed and ignorant, and so clearly unaware what the solution was, that the old lady burst into shrill, gay laughter as she looked at him.

"I don't believe you know anything about it," she said. "Are they old or young? are they pretty or ugly? Tell me all about them, Morley."

Now Mr Proctor had not the excuse of having forgotten the appearance of the two Miss Wodehouses: on the contrary, though not an imaginative man, he could have fancied he saw them both before him—Lucy lost in noiseless laughter, and her good elder sister deprecating and gentle as usual. We will not even undertake to say that a gleam of something blue did not flash across the mind of the good man, who did not know what ribbons were. He was so much bewildered that Mrs Proctor repeated her question, and, as she did so, tapped him pretty smartly on the arm to recall his wandering thoughts.

"One's one thing," at last shouted the confused man, "and t'other's another!" An oracular deliverance which surely must have been entirely unintelligible in the kitchen, where we will not deny that an utterance so incomprehensible awoke a laudable curiosity.

"My dear, you're lucid!" cried the old lady, "I hope you don't preach like that. T'other's another!—is she so? and I suppose that's the one you're wanted to marry—eh? For shame, Morley, not to tell your mother!"

The Rector jumped to his feet, thunderstruck. Wanted to marry!—the idea was too overwhelming and dreadful—his mind could not receive it. The air of alarm which immediately diffused itself all over him—his unfeigned horror at the suggestion—captivated his mother. She was amused, but she was pleased at the same time. Just making her cheery outset on this second lifetime, you can't suppose she would have been glad to hear that her son was going to jilt her, and appoint another queen in her stead.

"Sit down and tell me about them," said Mrs Proctor; "my dear, you're wonderfully afraid of the servants hearing. They don't know who we're speaking of. Aha! and so you didn't know what they meant—didn't you? I don't say you shouldn't marry, my dear—quite the reverse. A man ought to marry, one time or another. Only it's rather soon to lay their plans. I don't doubt there's a great many unmarried ladies in your church, Morley. There always is in a country place."

To this the alarmed Rector answered only by a groan—a groan so expressive that his quick-witted mother heard it with her eyes.

"They will come to call on me," said Mrs Proctor, with fun dancing in her bright old eyes. "I'll tell you all about them, and you needn't be afraid of the servants. Trust to me, my dear—I'll find them out. And now, if you wish to take a walk, or go out visiting, don't let me detain you, Morley. I shouldn't wonder but there's something in the papers I would like to see—or I even might close my eyes for a few minutes: the afternoon is always a drowsy time with me. When I was in Devonshire, you know, no one minded what I did. You had better refresh yourself with a nice walk, my dear boy."

The Rector got up well pleased. The alacrity with which he left the room, however, did not correspond with the horror-stricken and helpless expression of his face, when, after walking very smartly all round the Rectory garden, he paused with his hand on the gate, doubtful whether to retreat into his study, or boldly to face that world which was plotting against him. The question was a profoundly serious one to Mr Proctor. He did not feel by any means sure that he was a free agent, or could assert the ordinary rights of an Englishman, in this most unexpected dilemma. How could he tell how much or how little was necessary to prove that a man had "committed himself"? For anything he could tell, somebody might be calculating upon him as her lover, and settling his future life for him. The Rector was not vain—he did not think himself an Adonis; he did not understand anything about the matter, which indeed was beneath the consideration of a Fellow of All-Souls. But have not women been incomprehensible since ever there was in this world a pen with sufficient command of words to call them so? And is it not certain that, whether it may be to their advantage or disadvantage, every soul of them is plotting to marry somebody? Mr Proctor recalled in dim but frightful reminiscences stories which had dropped upon his ear at various times of his life. Never was there a man, however ugly, disagreeable, or penniless, but he could tell of a narrow escape he had, some time or other. The Rector recollected and trembled. No woman was ever so dismayed by the persecutions of a lover, as was this helpless middle-aged gentleman under the conviction that Lucy Wodehouse meant to marry him. The remembrance of the curate of St Roque's gave him no comfort: her sweet youth, so totally unlike his sober age, did not strike him as unfavourable to her pursuit of him. Who could fathom the motives of a woman? His mother was wise, and knew the world, and understood what such creatures meant. No doubt it was entirely the case—a dreadful certainty—and what was he to do?

At the bottom of all this fright and perplexity must it be owned that the Rector had a guilty consciousness within himself, that if Lucy drove the matter to extremities, he was not so sure of his own powers of resistance as he ought to be? She might marry him before he knew what he was about; and in such a case the Rector could not have taken his oath at his own private confessional that he would have been so deeply miserable as the circumstances might infer. No wonder he was alarmed at the position in which he found himself; nobody could predict how it might end.

When Mr Proctor saw his mother again at dinner, she was evidently full of some subject which would not bear talking of before the servants. The old lady looked at her son's troubled apprehensive face with smiles and nods and gay hints, which he was much too preoccupied to understand, and which only increased his bewilderment. When the good man was left alone over his glass of wine, he drank it slowly, in funereal silence, with profoundly serious looks; and what between eagerness to understand what the old lady meant, and reluctance to show the extent of his curiosity, had a very heavy half-hour of it in that grave solitary dining-room. He roused himself with an effort from this dismal state into which he was falling. He recalled with a sigh the classic board of All-Souls. Woe for the day when he was seduced to forsake that dear retirement! Really, to suffer himself to fall into a condition so melancholy, was far from being right. He must rouse himself—he must find some other society than parishioners;

and with a glimpse of a series of snug little dinner-parties, undisturbed by the presence of women, Mr Proctor rose and hurried after his mother, to hear what new thing she might have to say.

Nor was he disappointed. The old lady was snugly posted, ready for a conference. She made lively gestures to hasten him when he appeared at the door, and could scarcely delay the utterance of her news till he had taken his seat beside her. She had taken off her spectacles, and laid aside her paper, and cleared off her work into her work-basket. All was ready for the talk in which she delighted.

"My dear, they've been here," said old Mrs Proctor, rubbing her hands—"both together, and as kind as could be—exactly as I expected. An old woman gets double the attention when she's got an unmarried son. I've always observed that; though in Devonshire, what with your fellowship and seeing you so seldom, nobody took much notice. Yes, they've been here; and I like them a great deal better than I expected, Morley, my dear."

The Rector, not knowing what else to say, shouted "Indeed, mother!" into the old lady's ear.

"Quite so," continued that lively observer—"nice young women—not at all like their father, which is a great consolation. That elder one is a very sensible person, I am sure. She would make a nice wife for somebody, especially for a clergyman. She is not in her first youth, but neither are some other people. A very nice creature indeed, I am quite sure."

During all this speech the Rector's countenance had been falling, falling. If he was helpless before, the utter woe of his expression now was a spectacle to behold. The danger of being married by proxy was appalling certainly, yet was not entirely without alleviations; but Miss Wodehouse! who ever thought of Miss Wodehouse? To see the last remains of colour fade out of his cheek, and his very lip fall with disappointment, was deeply edifying to his lively old mother. She perceived it all, but made no sign.

"And the other is a pretty creature—certainly pretty: shouldn't you say she was pretty, Morley?" said his heartless mother.

Mr Proctor hesitated, hemmed—felt himself growing red—tried to intimate his sentiments by a nod of assent; but that would not do, for the old lady had presented her ear to him, and was blind to all his gestures.

"I don't know much about it, mother," he made answer at last.

"Much about it! it's to be hoped not. I never supposed you did; but you don't mean to say you don't think her pretty?" said Mrs Proctor—"but, I don't doubt in the least, a sad flirt. Her sister is a very superior person, my dear."

The Rector's face lengthened at every word—a vision of these two Miss Wodehouses rose upon him every moment clearer and more distinct as his mother spoke. Considering how ignorant he was of all such female paraphernalia, it is extraordinary how correct his recollection was of all the details of their habitual dress and appearance. With a certain dreadful consciousness of the justice of what his mother said, he saw in imagination the mild elder sister in her comely old-maidenhood. Nobody could doubt her good qualities, and could it be questioned that for a man of fifty, if he was to do anything so foolish, a woman not quite forty was a thousand times more eligible than a creature in blue ribbons? Still the unfortunate Rector did not seem to see it: his face grew longer and longer—he made no answer whatever to his mother's address; while she, with a spice of natural female malice against the common enemy triumphing for the moment over the mother's admiration of her son, sat wickedly enjoying his distress, and aggravating it. His dismay and perplexity amused this wicked old woman beyond measure.

"I have no doubt that younger girl takes a pleasure in deluding her admirers," said Mrs Proctor; "she's a wicked little flirt, and likes nothing better than to see her power. I know very well how such people do; but, my dear," continued this false old lady, scarcely able to restrain her laughter, "if I were you, I would be very civil to Miss Wodehouse. You may depend upon it, Morley, that's a very superior person. She is not very young, to be sure, but you are not very young yourself. She would make a nice wife—not too foolish, you know, nor fanciful. Ah! I like Miss Wodehouse, my dear."

The Rector stumbled up to his feet hastily, and pointed to a table at a little distance, on which some books were lying. Then he went and brought them to her table. "I've brought you some new books," he shouted into her ear. It was the only way his clumsy ingenuity could fall upon for bringing this most distasteful conversation to an end.

The old lady's eyes were dancing with fun and a little mischief, but, notwithstanding, she could not be so false to her nature as to show no interest in the books. She turned them over with lively remarks and comment. "But for all that, Morley, I would not have you forget Miss Wodehouse," she said, when her early bedtime came. "Give it a thought now and then, and consider the whole matter. It is not a thing to be done rashly; but still you know you are settled now, and you ought to be thinking of settling for life."

With this parting shaft she left him. The troubled Rector, instead of sitting up to his beloved studies, went early to bed that night, and was pursued by nightmares through his unquiet slumbers. Settling for life! Alas! there floated before him vain visions of that halcyon world he had left—that sacred soil at All-Souls, where there were no parishioners to break the sweet repose. How different was this discomposing real world!

CHAPTER III

Matters went on quietly for some time without any catastrophe occurring to the Rector. He had shut himself up from all society, and declined the invitations of the parishioners for ten long days at least; but finding that the kind people were only kinder than ever when they understood he was "indisposed," poor Mr Proctor resumed his ordinary life, confiding timidly in some extra precautions which his own ingenuity had invented. He was shyer than ever of addressing the ladies in those parties he was obliged to attend. He was especially embarrassed and uncomfortable in the presence of the two Miss Wodehouses, who, unfortunately, were very popular in Carlingford, and whom he could not help meeting everywhere. Notwithstanding this embarrassment, it is curious how well he knew how they looked, and what they were doing, and all about them. Though he could not for his life have told what these things were called, he knew Miss Wodehouse's dove-coloured dress and her French grey; and all those gleams of blue which set off Lucy's fair curls, and floated about her pretty person under various pretences, had a distinct though inarticulate place in the good man's confused remembrance. But neither Lucy nor Miss Wodehouse had brought matters to extremity. He even ventured to go to their house occasionally without any harm coming of it, and lingered in that blooming fragrant garden, where the blossoms had given place to fruit, and ruddy apples hung heavy on the branches which had once scattered their petals, rosy-white, on Frank Wentworth's Anglican coat. Yet Mr Proctor was not lulled into incaution by this seeming calm. Other people besides his mother had intimated to him that there were expectations current of his "settling in life." He lived not in false security, but wise trembling, never knowing what hour the thunderbolt might fall upon his head.

It happened one day, while still in this condition of mind, that the Rector was passing through Grove Street on his way home. He was walking on the humbler side of the street, where there is a row of cottages with little gardens in front of them—cheap houses, which are contented to be haughtily overlooked by the staircase windows and blank walls of their richer neighbours on the other side of the road. The Rector thought, but could not be sure, that he had seen two figures like those of the Miss Wodehouses going into one of these houses, and was making a little haste to escape meeting those enemies of his peace. But as he wont hastily on, he heard sobs and screams—sounds which a man who hid a good heart under a shy exterior could not willingly pass by. He made a troubled pause before the door from which these outcries proceeded, and while he stood thus irresolute whether to pass on or to stop and inquire the cause, some one came rushing out and took hold of his arm. "Please, sir, she's dying—oh, please, sir, she thought a deal o' you. Please, will you come in and speak to her?" cried the little servant-girl who had pounced upon him so. The Rector stared at her in amazement. He had not his prayer-book—he was not prepared; he had no idea of being called upon in such an emergency. In the mean time the commotion rather increased in the house, and he could hear in the distance a voice adjuring some one to go for the clergyman. The Rector stood uncertain and perplexed, perhaps in a more serious personal difficulty than had ever happened to him all his life before. For what did he know about deathbeds? or what had he to say to any one on that dread verge? He grew pale with real vexation and distress.

"Have they gone for a doctor? that would be more to the purpose," he said, unconsciously, aloud.

"Please, sir, it's no good," said the little maid-servant. "Please, the doctor's been, but he's no good—and she's unhappy in her mind, though she's quite resigned to go: and oh, please, if you would say a word to her, it might do her a deal of good."

Thus adjured, the Rector had no choice. He went gloomily into the house and up the stair after his little guide. Why did not they send for the minister of Salem Chapel close by? or for Mr Wentworth, who was accustomed to that sort of thing? Why did they resort to him in such an emergency? He would have made his appearance before the highest magnates of the land—before the Queen herself—before the bench of bishops or the Privy Council—with less trepidation than he entered that poor little room.

The sufferer lay breathing heavily in the poor apartment. She did not look very ill to Mr Proctor's inexperienced eyes. Her colour was bright, and her face full of eagerness. Near the door stood Miss Wodehouse, looking compassionate but helpless, casting wistful glances at the bed, but standing back in a corner as confused and embarrassed as the Rector himself. Lucy was standing by the pillow of the sick woman with a watchful readiness visible to the most unskilled eye—ready to raise her, to change her position, to attend to her wants almost before they were expressed. The contrast was wonderful. She had thrown off her bonnet and shawl, and appeared, not like a stranger, but somehow in her natural place, despite the sweet youthful beauty of her looks, and the gay girlish dress with its floating ribbons. These singular adjuncts notwithstanding, no homely nurse in a cotton gown could have looked more alert or serviceable, or more natural to the position, than Lucy did. The poor Rector, taking the seat which the little maid placed for him directly in the centre of the room, looked at the nurse and the patient with a gasp of perplexity and embarrassment. A deathbed, alas! was an unknown region to him.

"Oh, sir, I'm obliged to you for coming—oh, sir, I'm grateful to you," cried the poor woman in the bed. "I've been ill, off and on, for years, but never took thought to it as I ought. I've put off and put off, waiting for a better time—and now, God help me, it's perhaps too late. Oh, sir, tell me, when a person's ill and dying, is it too late?"

Before the Rector could even imagine what he could answer, the sick woman took up the broken thread of her own words, and continued—

"I don't feel to trust as I ought to—I don't feel no confidence," she said, in anxious confession. "Oh, sir, do you think it matters if one feels it?—don't you think things might be right all the same though we were uneasy in our minds? My thinking can't change it one way or another. Ask the good gentleman to speak to me, Miss Lucy, dear—he'll mind what you say."

A look from Lucy quickened the Rector's speech, but increased his embarrassments. "It—it isn't her doctor she has no confidence in?" he said, eagerly.

The poor woman gave a little cry. "The doctor—the doctor! what can he do to a poor dying creature? Oh, Lord bless you, it's none of them things I'm thinking of; it's my soul—my soul!"

"But my poor good woman," said Mr Proctor, "though it is very good and praiseworthy of you to be anxious about your soul, let us hope that there is no such—no such haste as you seem to suppose."

The patient opened her eyes wide, and stared, with the anxious look of disease, in his face.

"I mean," said the good man, faltering under that gaze, "that I see no reason for your making yourself so very anxious. Let us hope it is not so bad as that. You are very ill, but not so ill—I suppose."

Here the Rector was interrupted by a groan from the patient, and by a troubled, disapproving, disappointed look from Lucy Wodehouse. This brought him to a sudden standstill. He gazed for a moment helplessly at the poor woman in the bed. If he had known anything in the world which would have given her consolation, he was ready to have made any exertion for it; but he knew nothing to say—no medicine for a mind diseased was in his repositories. He was deeply distressed to see the disappointment which followed his words, but his distress only made him more silent, more helpless, more inefficient than before.

After an interval which was disturbed only by the groans of the patient and the uneasy fidgeting of good Miss Wodehouse in her corner, the Rector again broke silence. The sick woman had turned to the wall, and closed her eyes in dismay and disappointment—evidently she had ceased to expect anything from him.

"If there is anything I can do," said poor Mr Proctor, "I am afraid I have spoken hastily. I meant to try to calm her mind a little; if I can be of any use?"

"Ah, maybe I'm hasty," said the dying woman, turning round again with a sudden effort—"but, oh, to speak to me of having time when I've one foot in the grave already!"

"Not so bad as that—not so bad as that," said the Rector, soothingly.

"But I tell you it is as bad as that," she cried, with the brief blaze of anger common to great weakness. "I'm not a child to be persuaded different from what I know. If you'd tell me—if you'd say a prayer—ah, Miss Lucy, it's coming on again."

In a moment Lucy had raised the poor creature in her arms, and in default of the pillows which were not at hand, had risen herself into their place, and supported the gasping woman against her own breast. It was a paroxysm dreadful to behold, in which every labouring breath seemed the last. The Rector sat like one struck dumb, looking on at that mortal struggle. Miss Wodehouse approached nervously from behind, and went up to the bedside, faltering forth questions as to what she could do. Lucy only waved her hand, as her own light figure swayed and changed, always seeking the easiest attitude for the sufferer. As the elder sister drew back, the Rector and she glanced at each other with wistful mutual looks of sympathy. Both were equally well-disposed, equally helpless and embarrassed. How to be of any use in that dreadful agony of nature was denied to both. They stood looking on, awed and self-reproaching. Such scenes have doubtless happened in sick-rooms before now.

When the fit was over, a hasty step came up the stair, and Mr Wentworth entered the room. He explained in a whisper that he had not been at home when the messenger came, but had followed whenever he heard of the message. Seeing the Rector, he hesitated, and drew back with some surprise, and, even (for he was far from perfect) in that chamber, a little flush of offence. The Rector rose abruptly, waving his hand, and went to join Miss Wodehouse in her corner. There the two elderly spectators looked on silent at ministrations of which both were incapable; one watching with wondering yet affectionate envy how Lucy laid down the weakened but relieved patient upon her pillows; and one beholding with a surprise he could not conceal, how a young man, not half his own age, went softly, with all the confidence yet awe of nature, into those mysteries which he dared not touch upon. The two young creatures by the deathbed acknowledged that their patient was dying; the woman stood by her watchful and affectionate—the man held up before her that cross, not of wood or metal, but of truth and everlasting verity, which is the only hope of man. The spectators looked on, and did not interrupt—looked on, awed and wondering—unaware of how it was, but watching, as if it were a miracle wrought before their eyes. Perhaps all the years of his life had not taught the Rector so much as did that half-hour in an unknown poor bed-chamber, where, honest and humble, he stood aside, and, kneeling down, responded to his young brother's prayer. His young brother—young enough to have been his son—not half nor a quarter part so learned as he; but a world further on in that profession which they shared—the art of winning souls.

When those prayers were over, the Rector, without a word to anybody, stole quietly away. When he got into the street, however, he found himself closely followed by Miss Wodehouse, of whom he was not at this moment afraid. That good creature was crying softly under her veil. She was eager to make up to him, to open out her full heart; and indeed the Rector, like herself, in that wonderful sensation of surprised and unenvying discomfiture, was glad at that moment of sympathy too.

"Oh, Mr Proctor, isn't it wonderful?" sighed good Miss Wodehouse.

The Rector did not speak, but he answered by a very emphatic nod of his head.

"It did not use to be so when you and I were young," said his companion in failure. "I sometimes take a little comfort from that; but no doubt, if it had been in me, it would have shown itself somehow. Ah, I fear, I fear, I was not well brought up; but, to be sure, that dear child has not been brought up at all, if one may say so. Her poor mother died when she was born. And oh, I'm afraid I never was kind to Lucy's mother, Mr Proctor. You know she was only a year or two older than I was; and to think of that child, that baby! What a world she is, and always was, before me, that might have been her mother, Mr Proctor!" said Miss Wodehouse, with a little sob.

"But things were different in our young days," said the Rector, repeating her sentiment, without inquiring whether it were true or not, and finding a certain vague consolation in it.

"Ah, that is true," said Miss Wodehouse—"that is true; what a blessing things are so changed; and these blessed young creatures," she added softly, with tears falling out of her gentle old eyes—"these blessed young creatures are near the Fountainhead."

With this speech Miss Wodehouse held out her hand to the Rector, and they parted with a warm mutual grasp. The Rector went straight home—straight to his study, where he shut himself in, and was not to be disturbed; that night was one long to be remembered in the good man's history. For the first time in his life he set himself to inquire what was his supposed business in this world. His treatise on the Greek verb, and his new edition of Sophocles, were highly creditable to the Fellow of All-Souls; but how about the Rector of Carlingford? What was he doing here, among that little world of human creatures who were dying, being born, perishing, suffering, falling into misfortune and anguish, and all manner of human vicissitudes, every day? Young Wentworth knew what to say to that woman in her distress; and so might the Rector, had her distress concerned a disputed translation, or a disused idiom. The good man was startled in his composure and calm. To-day he had visibly failed in a duty which even in All-Souls was certainly known to be one of the duties of a Christian priest. Was he a Christian priest, or what was he? He was troubled to the very depths of his soul. To hold an office the duties of which he could not perform, was clearly impossible. The only question, and that a hard one, was, whether he could learn to discharge those duties, or whether he must cease to be Rector of Carlingford. He laboured over this problem in his solitude, and could find no answer. "Things were different when we were young," was the only thought that was any comfort to him, and that was poor consolation.

For one thing, it is hard upon the most magnanimous of men to confess that he has undertaken an office for which he has not found himself capable. Magnanimity was perhaps too lofty a word to apply to the Rector; but he was honest to the bottom of his soul. As soon as he became aware of what was included in the duties of his office, he must perform them, or quit his post. But how to perform them? Can one learn to convey consolation to the dying, to teach the ignorant, to comfort the sorrowful? Are these matters to be acquired by study, like Greek verbs or intricate measures? The Rector's heart said No. The Rector's imagination unfolded before him, in all its halcyon blessedness, that ancient paradise of All-Souls, where no such confounding demands ever disturbed his beatitude. The good man groaned within himself over the mortification, the labour, the sorrow, which this living was bringing upon him. "If I had but let it pass to Morgan, who wanted to marry," he said with self-reproach; and then suddenly bethought himself of his own most innocent filial romance, and the pleasure his mother had taken in her new house and new beginning of life. At that touch the tide flowed back again. Could he dismiss her now to another solitary cottage in Devonshire, her old home there being all dispersed and broken up, while the house she had hoped to die in cast her out from its long-hoped-for shelter? The Rector was quite overwhelmed by this new aggravation. If by any effort of his own, any sacrifice to himself, he could preserve this bright new home to his mother, would he shrink from that labour of love?

Nobody, however, knew anything about those conflicting thoughts which rent his sober bosom. He preached next Sunday as usual, letting no trace of the distressed, wistful anxiety to do his duty which now possessed him gleam into his sermon. He looked down upon a crowd of unsympathetic, uninterested faces, when he delivered that smooth little sermon, which nobody cared much about, and which disturbed nobody. The only eyes which in the smallest degree comprehended him were those of good Miss Wodehouse, who had been the witness and the participator of his humiliation. Lucy was not there. Doubtless Lucy was at St Roque's, where the sermons of the perpetual curate differed much from those of the Rector of Carlingford. Ah me! the rectorship, with all its responsibilities, was a serious business; and what was to become of it yet, Mr Proctor could not see. He was not a hasty man—he determined to wait and see what events might make of it; to consider it ripely—to take full counsel with himself. Every time he came out of his mother's presence, he came affected and full of anxiety to preserve to her that home which pleased her so much. She was the strong point in favour of Carlingford; and it was no small tribute to the good man's filial affection, that for her chiefly he kept his neck under the yoke of a service to which he knew himself unequal, and, sighing, turned his back upon his beloved cloisters. If there had been no other sick-beds immediately in Carlingford, Mrs Proctor would have won the day.

CHAPTER IV

Such a blessed exemption, however, was not to be hoped for. When the Rector was solemnly sent for from his very study to visit a poor man who was not expected to live many days, he put his prayer-book under his arm, and went off doggedly, feeling that now was the crisis. He went through it in as exemplary a manner as could have been desired, but it was dreadful work to the Rector. If nobody else suspected him, he suspected himself. He had no spontaneous word of encouragement or consolation to offer; he went through it as his duty with a horrible abstractness. That night he went home disgusted beyond all possible power of self-reconciliation. He could not continue this. Good evangelical Mr Bury, who went before him, and by nature loved preaching, had accustomed the people to much of such visitations. It was murder to the Fellow of All-Souls.

That night Mr Proctor wrote a long letter to his dear cheery old mother, disclosing all his heart to her. It was written with a pathos of which the good man was wholly unconscious, and finished by asking her advice and her prayers. He sent it up to her next morning on her breakfast tray, which he always furnished with his own hands, and went out to occupy himself in paying visits till it should be time to see her, and ascertain her opinion. At Mr Wodehouse's there was nobody at home but Lucy, who was very friendly, and took no notice of that sad encounter which had changed his views so entirely. The Rector found, on inquiry, that the woman was dead, but not until Mr Wentworth had administered to her fully the consolations of the church. Lucy did not look superior, or say anything in admiration of Mr Wentworth, but the Rector's conscience supplied all that was wanting. If good Miss Wodehouse had been there with her charitable looks, and her dis-efficiency so like his own, it would have been a consolation to the good man. He would have turned joyfully from Lucy and her blue ribbons to that distressed dove-coloured woman, so greatly had recent events changed him. But the truth was, he cared nothing for either of them nowadays. He was delivered from those whimsical distressing fears. Something more serious had obliterated those lighter apprehensions. He had no leisure now to think that somebody had planned to marry him; all his thoughts were fixed on matters so much more important that this was entirely forgotten.

Mrs Proctor was seated as usual in the place she loved, with her newspapers, her books, her work-basket, and silver-headed cane at the side of her chair. The old lady, like her son, looked serious. She beckoned him to quicken his steps when she saw him appear at the drawing-room door, and pointed to the chair placed beside her, all ready for this solemn conference. He came in with a troubled face, scarcely venturing to look at her, afraid to see the disappointment which he had brought upon his dearest friend. The old lady divined why it was he did not lift his eyes. She took his hand and addressed him with all her characteristic vivacity.

"Morley, what is this you mean, my dear? When did I ever give my son reason to distrust me? Do you think I would suffer you to continue in a position painful to yourself for my sake? How dare you think such a thing of me, Morley? Don't say so? you didn't mean it; I can see it in your eyes."

The Rector shook his head, and dropped into the chair placed ready for him. He might have had a great deal to say for himself could she have heard him. But as it was, he could not shout all his reasons and apologies into her deaf ear.

"As for the change to me," said the old lady, instinctively seizing upon the heart of the difficulty, "that's nothing—simply nothing. I've not had time to get attached to Carlingford. I've no associations with the place. Of course I shall be very glad to go back to all my old friends. Put that out of the question, Morley."

But the Rector only shook his head once more. The more she made light of it, the more he perceived all the painful circumstances involved. Could his mother go back to Devonshire and tell all her old ladies that her son had made a failure in Carlingford? He grieved within himself at the thought. His brethren at All-Souls might understand him; but what could console the brave old woman for all the condolence and commiseration to which she would be subject? "It goes to my heart, mother," he cried in her ear.

"Well, Morley, I am very sorry you find it so," said the old lady; "very sorry you can't see your way to all your duties. They tell me the late rector was very Low Church, and visited about like a Dissenter, so it is not much wonder you, with your different habits, find yourself a good deal put out; but, my dear, don't you think it's only at first? Don't you think after a while the people would get into your ways, and you into theirs? Miss Wodehouse was here this morning, and was telling me a good deal about the late rector. It's to be expected you should find the difference; but by-and-by, to be sure, you might get used to it, and the people would not expect so much."

"Did she tell you where we met the other day?" asked the Rector, with a brevity rendered necessary by Mrs Proctor's infirmity.

"She told me—she's a dear confused good soul," said the old lady—"about the difference between Lucy and herself, and how the young creature was twenty times handier than she, and something about young Mr Wentworth of St Roque's. Really, by all I hear, that must be a very presuming young man," cried Mrs Proctor, with a lively air of offence. "His interference among your parishioners, Morley, is really more than I should be inclined to bear."

Once more the good Rector shook his head. He had not thought of that aspect of the subject. He was indeed so free from vanity or self-importance, that his only feeling in regard to the sudden appearance of the perpetual curate was respect and surprise. He would not be convinced otherwise even now. "He can do his duty, mother," he answered, sadly.

"Stuff and nonsense!" cried the old lady. "Do you mean to tell me a boy like that can do his duty better than my son could do it, if he put his mind to it? And if it is your duty, Morley, dear," continued his mother, melting a little, and in a coaxing persuasive tone, "of course I know you will do it, however hard it may be."

"That's just the difficulty," cried the Rector, venturing on a longer speech than usual, and roused to a point at which he had no fear of the listeners in the kitchen; "such duties require other training than mine has been. I can't!—do you hear me, mother?—I must not hold a false position; that's impossible."

"You shan't hold a false position," cried the old lady; "that's the only thing that is impossible—but, Morley, let us consider, dear. You are a clergyman, you know; you ought to understand all that's required of you a great deal better than these people do. My dear, your poor father and I trained you up to be a clergyman," said Mrs Proctor, rather pathetically, "and not to be a Fellow of All-Souls."

The Rector groaned. Had it not been advancement, progress, unhoped-for good fortune, that made him a member of that learned corporation? He shook his head. Nothing could change the fact now. After fifteen years' experience of that Elysium, he could not put on the cassock and surplice with all his youthful fervour. He had settled into his life-habits long ago. With the quick perception which made up for her deficiency, his mother read his face, and saw the cause was hopeless; yet with female courage and pertinacity made one effort more.

"And with an excellent hard-working curate," said the old lady—"a curate whom, of course, we'd do our duty by, Morley, and who could take a great deal of the responsibility off your hands; for Mr Leigh, though a nice young man, is not, I know, the man you would have chosen for such a post; and still more, my dear son—we were talking of it in jest not long ago, but it is perfect earnest, and a most important matter—with a good wife, Morley; a wife who would enter into all the parish work, and give you useful hints, and conduct herself as a clergyman's wife should—with such a wife—"

"Lucy Wodehouse!" cried the Rector, starting to his feet, and forgetting all his proprieties; "I tell you the thing is impossible. I'll go back to All-Souls."

He sat down again doggedly, having said it. His mother sat looking at him in silence, with tears in her lively old eyes. She was saying within herself that she had seen his father take just such a "turn," and that it was no use arguing with them under such circumstances. She watched him as women often do watch men, waiting till the creature should come to itself again and might be spoken to. The incomprehensibleness of women is an old theory, but what is that to the curious wondering observation with which wives, mothers, and sisters watch the other unreasoning animal in those moments when he has snatched the reins out of their hands, and is not to be spoken to! What he will make of it in those unassisted moments, afflicts the compassionate female understanding. It is best to let him come to, and feel his own helplessness. Such was Mrs Proctor's conclusion, as, vexed, distressed, and helpless, she leant back in her chair, and wiped a few tears of disappointment and vexation out of her bright old eyes.

The Rector saw this movement, and it once more excited him to speech. "But you shall have a house in Oxford, mother," he cried—"you shan't go back to Devonshire—where I can see you every day, and you can hear all that is going on. Bravo! that will be a thousand times better than Carlingford."

It was now Mrs Proctor's turn to jump up, startled, and put her hand on his mouth and point to the door. The Rector did not care for the door; he had disclosed his sentiments, he had taken his resolution, and now the sooner all was over the better for the emancipated man.

Thus concluded the brief incumbency of the Reverend Morley Proctor. He returned to Oxford before his year of grace was over, and found everybody very glad to see him; and he left Carlingford with universal good wishes. The living fell to Morgan, who wanted to be married, and whose turn was much more to be a working clergyman than a classical commentator. Old Mrs Proctor got a pretty house under shelter of the trees of St Giles's, and half the under-graduates fell in love with the old lady in the freshness of her second lifetime. Carlingford passed away like a dream from the lively old mother's memory, and how could any reminiscences of that uncongenial locality disturb the recovered beatitude of the Fellow of All-Souls?

Yet all was not so satisfactory as it appeared. Mr Proctor paid for his temporary absence. All-Souls was not the Elysium it had been before that brief disastrous voyage into the world. The good man felt the stings of failure; he felt the mild jokes of his brethren in those Elysian fields. He could not help conjuring up to himself visions of Morgan with his new wife in that pretty rectory. Life, after all, did not consist of books, nor were Greek verbs essential to happiness. The strong emotion into which his own failure had roused him; the wondering silence in which he stood looking at the ministrations of Lucy Wodehouse and the young curate; the tearful sympathetic woman as helpless as himself, who had stood beside him in that sick chamber, came back upon his recollection strangely, amidst the repose, not so blessed as heretofore, of All-Souls. The good man had found out that secret of discontent which most men find out a great deal earlier than he. Something better, though it might be sadder, harder, more calamitous, was in this world. Was there ever human creature yet that had not something in him more congenial to the thorns and briars outside to be conquered, than to that mild paradise for which our primeval mother disqualified all her children? When he went back to his dear cloisters, good Mr Proctor felt that sting: a longing for the work he had rejected stirred in him—a wistful recollection of the sympathy he had not sought.

And if in future years any traveller, if travellers still fall upon adventures, should light upon a remote parsonage in which an elderly embarrassed Rector, with a mild wife in dove-coloured dresses, toils painfully after his duty, more and more giving his heart to it, more and more finding difficult expression for the unused faculty, let him be sure that it is the late Rector of Carlingford, self-expelled out of the uneasy paradise, setting forth untimely, yet not too late, into the laborious world.

Margaret Oliphant – A Short Biography

Margaret Oliphant Wilson was born on April 4th, 1828 to Francis W. Wilson, a clerk, and Margaret Oliphant, at Wallyford, near Musselburgh, East Lothian.

She spent her childhood at Lasswade, near Dalkeith, Glasgow before moving to Liverpool.

Her youth was spent in establishing a writing style so much so that, in 1849, she had her first novel published: Passages in the Life of Mrs. Margaret Maitland based on the Scottish Free Church movement. It met with some success and was a good start to her career.

Two years later, in 1851, her third book Caleb Field was published. It was also now that she met the publisher William Blackwood in Edinburgh and was asked to contribute to his well-received Blackwood's Magazine. It was to be a lifetimes endeavor. Over the course of the relationship she would have well over 100 articles published.

In May 1852, Margaret married her cousin, Frank Wilson Oliphant, at Birkenhead, and they settled at Harrington Square, Camden, London. He was an artist working primarily in stained glass. With the marriage she became Margaret Oliphant Wilson Oliphant.

Their marriage produced six children but three tragically died in infancy.

When her husband developed signs of the dreaded consumption (tuberculosis) they moved, on the advice of doctors, to warmer climes. In January 1859 it was to Florence, and then to Rome where, sadly, he died.

Margaret was naturally devastated but was also now left without support and only her income from her writing. She returned to England and took up the task of supporting her three remaining children by her literary activity.

By now she was being published both as an established novelist and regularly in Blackwood's Magazine, amongst others. Her incredible and prolific work rate increased both her commercial reputation and the size of her reading audience.

Against this her domestic life continued to be tragic, full of sorrow and disappointment.

In January 1864 her only remaining daughter Maggie died and was buried in her father's grave in Rome. Her brother, who had emigrated to Canada, was shortly afterwards involved in financial ruin. Margaret generously offered a home to him and his children, adding another demand to her already heavy responsibilities.

In 1866 she settled at Windsor to be closer to her sons, who were being educated at near-by Eton School. That year, her second cousin, Annie Louisa Walker, came to live with her as a companion-housekeeper. Windsor was now to be her home for the rest of her life.

Her literary career for three decades was one of constant delivery and success. Whether she wrote historical works or across several genres in fiction: domestic realism, historical, romance or supernatural she was successful.

For more than thirty years she pursued a varied literary career but family life continued to bring problems.

The literary ambitions she wished for her sons were unfulfilled. Cyril Francis, the eldest, died in 1890, leaving a Life of Alfred de Musset, incorporated in his mother's Foreign Classics for English Readers. The younger, Francis, who she nicknamed 'Cecco', collaborated with her in the Victorian Age of English Literature and won a position at the British Museum, but was rejected by Sir Andrew Clark, a famous physician. Cecco died in 1894.

With the last of her children now lost to her, she had but little further interest in life. Her health steadily and inexorably declined.

Margaret Oliphant Wilson Oliphant died at the age of 69 in Wimbledon on 20th June 1897. She is buried in Eton beside her sons.

At her death, Margaret was still working on Annals of a Publishing House, a record of Blackwood's Magazine with which she had enjoyed such a successful relationship.

Her Autobiography and Letters, which present a thoughtful picture of her domestic anxieties, was published in 1899. Only parts were written with a wider audience in mind: she had originally intended the Autobiography for her son, but he died before she could finish it.

Opinions on Oliphant's work are split, with some critics seeing her as a 'domestic novelist', while others recognize her work as influential and important to the Victorian literature canon. Critical reception from her contemporaries is also divided. John Skelton took the view that Oliphant wrote too much and too quickly. Writing a Blackwood's article called 'A Little Chat About Mrs. Oliphant', he asked, "Had Mrs. Oliphant concentrated her powers, what might she not have done? We might have had another Charlotte Brontë or another George Eliot." However not all of the contemporary reception was negative. The esteemed M. R. James admired Oliphant's supernatural fiction, concluding that "the religious ghost story, as it may be called, was never done better than by Mrs. Oliphant in 'The Open Door' and 'A Beleaguered City'. Mary Butts lavished praise on Oliphant's ghost story 'The Library Window', describing it as "one masterpiece of sober loveliness".

More modern critics of Oliphant's work include Virginia Woolf, who asked in Three Guineas whether Oliphant's autobiography does not lead the reader "to deplore the fact that Mrs. Oliphant sold her brain, her very admirable brain, prostituted her culture and enslaved her intellectual liberty in order that she might earn her living and educate her children."

Whatever the merits of their cases Margaret Oliphant has been shamefully neglected in modern years. She is now becoming more widely recognised as a leading writer of her day.

Margaret Oliphant – A Concise Bibliography

A canon of more than 120 works, including novels, travel books, histories, and volumes of literary criticism.

Novels

Margaret Maitland (1849)
Merkland (1850)
Caleb Field (1851)
John Drayton (1851)
Adam Graeme (1852)
The Melvilles (1852)
Katie Stewart (1852)
Harry Muir (1853)
Ailieford (1853)
The Quiet Heart (1854)
Magdalen Hepburn (1854)
Zaidee (1855)

Lilliesleaf (1855)
Christian Melville (1855)
The Athelings (1857)
The Days of My Life (1857)
Orphans (1858)
The Laird of Norlaw (1858)
Agnes Hopetoun's Schools and Holidays (1859)
Lucy Crofton (1860)
The House on the Moor (1861)
The Last of the Mortimers (1862)
Heart and Cross (1863)
Salem Chapel (1863)
The Rector (1863)
Doctor's Family (1863)
The Perpetual Curate (1864)
Miss Marjoribanks (1866)
Phoebe Junior (1876)
A Son of the Soil (1865)
Agnes (1866)
Madonna Mary (1867)
Brownlows (1868)
The Minister's Wife (1869)
The Three Brothers (1870)
John: A Love Story (1870)
Squire Arden (1871)
At his Gates (1872)
Ombra (1872
May (1873)
Innocent (1873)
The Story of Valentine and his Brother (1875)
A Rose in June (1874)
For Love and Life (1874)
Whiteladies (1875)
An Odd Couple (1875)
The Curate in Charge (1876)
Carità (1877)
Young Musgrave (1877)
Mrs. Arthur (1877)
The Primrose Path (1878)
Within the Precincts (1879)
The Fugitives (1879)
A Beleaguered City (1879)
The Greatest Heiress in England (1880)
He That Will Not When He May (1880)
In Trust (1881)
Harry Joscelyn (1881)
Lady Jane (1882)
A Little Pilgrim in the Unseen (1882)

The Lady Lindores (1883)
Sir Tom (1883)
Hester (1883)
It Was a Lover and his Lass (1883)
The Lady's Walk (1883)
The Wizard's Son (1884)
Madam (1884)
The Prodigals and their Inheritance (1885)
Oliver's Bride (1885)
A Country Gentleman and his Family (1886)
A House Divided Against Itself (1886)
Effie Ogilvie (1886)
A Poor Gentleman (1886)
The Son of his Father (1886)
Joyce (1888)
Cousin Mary (1888)
The Land of Darkness (1888)
Lady Car (1889)
Kirsteen (1890)
The Mystery of Mrs. Biencarrow (1890)
Sons and Daughters (1890)
The Railway Man and his Children (1891)
The Heir Presumptive and the Heir Apparent (1891)
The Marriage of Elinor (1891)
Janet (1891)
The Cuckoo in the Nest (1892)
Diana Trelawny (1892)
The Sorceress (1893)
A House in Bloomsbury (1894)
Sir Robert's Fortune (1894)
Who Was Lost and is Found (1894)
Lady William (1894)
Two Strangers (1895)
Old Mr. Tredgold (1895)
The Unjust Steward (1896)
The Ways of Life (1897)

Short stories

Neighbours on the Green (1889)
A Widow's Tale and Other Stories (1898)
That Little Cutty (1898)
The Open Door (1918)

Selected Articles

Mary Russel Mitford (Blackwood's Magazine, Vol. 75, 1854)

Evelin and Pepys (Blackwood's Magazine, Vol. 76, 1854)
The Holy Land (Blackwood's Magazine, Vol. 76, 1854)
Mr. Thackeray and his Novels (Blackwood's Magazine, Vol. 77, 1855)
Bulwer (Blackwood's Magazine, Vol. 77, 1855)
Charles Dickens (Blackwood's Magazine, Vol. 77, 1855)
Modern Novelists—Great and Small (Blackwood's Magazine, Vol. 77, 1855)
Modern Light Literature: Poetry (Blackwood's Magazine, Vol. 79, 1856)
Religion in Common Life (Blackwood's Magazine, Vol. 79, 1856)
Sydney Smith (Blackwood's Magazine, Vol. 79, 1856)
The Laws Concerning Women (Blackwood's Magazine, Vol. 79, 1856)
The Art of Caviling (Blackwood's Magazine, Vol. 80, 1856)
Béranger (Blackwood's Magazine, Vol. 83, 1858)
The Condition of Women (Blackwood's Magazine, Vol. 83, 1858)
The Missionary Explorer (Blackwood's Magazine, Vol. 83, 1858)
Religious Memoirs (Blackwood's Magazine, Vol. 83, 1858)
Social Science (Blackwood's Magazine, Vol. 88, 1860)
Scotland and her Accusers (Blackwood's Magazine, Vol. 90, 1861)
The Chronicles of Carlingford (Blackwood's Magazine 1862–1865)
Girolamo Savonarola (Blackwood's Magazine, Vol. 93, 1863)
The Life of Jesus (Blackwood's Magazine, Vol. 96, 1864)
Giacomo Leopardi (Blackwood's Magazine, Vol. 98, 1865)
The Great Unrepresented (Blackwood's Magazine, Vol. 100, 1866)
Mill on the Subjection of Women (The Edinburgh Review, Vol. 130, 1869)
The Opium-Eater (Blackwood's Magazine, Vol. 122, 1877)
Russian and Nihilism in the Novels of I. Tourgeniéf (Blackwood's Magazine, Vol. 127, 1880)
School and College (Blackwood's Magazine, Vol. 128, 1880)
The Grievances of Women (Fraser's Magazine, New Series, Vol. 21, 1880)
Mrs. Carlyle (The Contemporary Review, Vol. 43, May 1883)
The Ethics of Biography (The Contemporary Review, July 1883)
Victor Hugo (The Contemporary Review, Vol. 48, July/December 1885)
A Venetian Dynasty (The Contemporary Review, Vol. 50, August 1886)
Laurence Oliphant (Blackwood's Magazine, Vol. 145, 1889)
Tennyson (Blackwood's Magazine, Vol. 152, 1892)
Addison, the Humorist (Century Magazine, Vol. 48, 1894)
The Anti-Marriage League (Blackwood's Magazine, Vol. 159, 1896)

Biographies

Edward Irving (1862)
Francis of Assisi (1871)
Count de Montalembert (1872)
Dante (1877)
Cervantes (1880)
Life of Sheridan in the English Men of Letters series (1883)
John Tulloch (1888)
Laurence Oliphant (1892)

Historical & Critical Works

Historical Sketches of the Reign of George II (1869)
The Makers of Florence (1876)
A Literary History of England from 1760 to 1825 (1882)
The Makers of Venice (1887)
Royal Edinburgh (1890)
Jerusalem (1891)
The Makers of Modern Rome (1895)
William Blackwood and his Sons (1897)
The Sisters Brontë. In: Women Novelists of Queen Victoria's Reign (1897)

ompliance